T0381016

The
SOUND
of
SAM

The Lost Note

Bethany Bateman

authorHOUSE

AuthorHouse™
1663 Liberty Drive
Bloomington, IN 47403
www.authorhouse.com
Phone: 833-262-8899

Published by AuthorHouse 10/24/2024

ISBN: 979-8-8230-3186-8 (sc)
ISBN: 979-8-8230-3185-1 (e)

Library of Congress Control Number: 2024920792

Print information available on the last page.

His name is Sam, and he is a quarter note.

He looks like this....

He came tumbling down from somewhere,
and he doesn't know how to get home.

Sam is a member of the very large music family, but right now
he can't remember where he belongs, or what he is supposed to do.
He knows his family is at home, and worried about him!

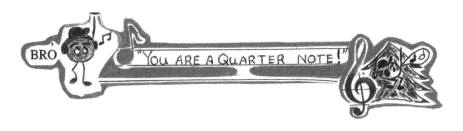

SAM started running along the sidewalk, and he saw some children playing. He ran up to them for help; they laughed, and said, "look at that little note ..What do you suppose he's doing here?"

SAM tried very hard to tell them, but, they couldn't hear him, and they ran off to play. SAM had made No sound.... No sound at all!

The Sound of Sam

But the owl looked at SAM,
Sitting there on the ground,
And he thought "This is sad.....
That poor note has NO SOUND!"

and Sam cried, "Oh dear!! I may never be found!"

The Sound of Sam

When he heard the happy sounds of a beautiful robin chirping; SAM tried to call out to him, but the robin didn't answer. SAM wondered why?

The church bells were ringing ♫; the birds were singing ♪; the Owl was hooting ♫; and the children were laughing ♪. These were "The sounds of music." "THE SOUNDS of SAM" He really wanted to talk and sing.

The Sound of Sam

SAM was very sad... why couldn't anyone hear him calling for help. He was getting very tired, but he had to keep looking. He couldn't find his SOUND, and he was lonely for his Mother and Father.

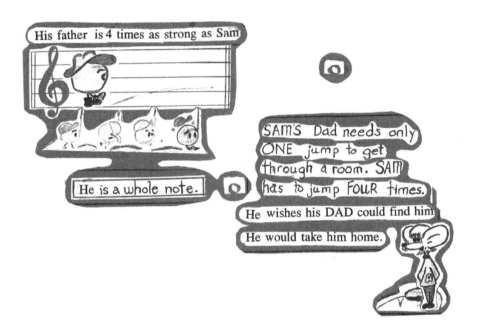

As he was searching, he wandered across

some railway tracks.

He trotted

along one of the tracks,

and began to hum... to himself.

"I like this," he thought happily.

"Maybe my family is at the other end"

Then he heard a train.
"What a huge sound", thought SAM. "If I could sound like that, my family would hear me for sure". The wheels were going clickety-click....clickety-click, and even though SAM was still shaking, he liked that sound too.

My brother and sisters would love this SouND, thought SAM.

Sam was frightened,
..it kept getting louder and louder....
and he jumped off the track,
just as the big train roared by.

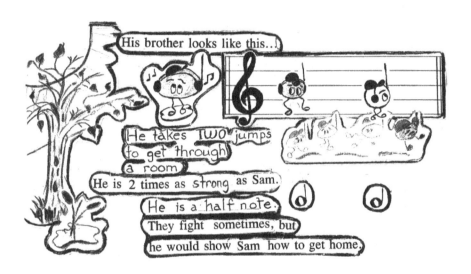

NO ONE COULD HEAR HIM!
but he didn't know why.

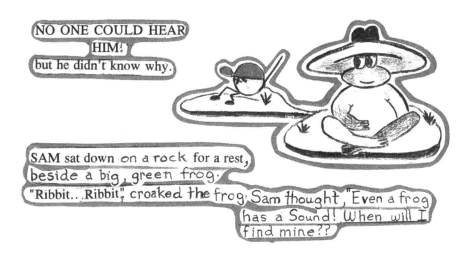

SAM sat down on a rock for a rest, beside a big, green frog.
"Ribbit... Ribbit," croaked the frog. Sam thought, "Even a frog has a Sound! When will I find mine??

Then a girl and boy came along, playing with a ball.

Then, they saw the frog ... and SAM.

The children thought Sam might be a bug, but the boy picked him up anyway.
"Look Paige it's a note"
She came very close, and held out her hand.
"Oh Trent He looks so sad and lost—
...let's take him home, to Mother and Father."

"Hooray", thought Sam. " Paige and Trent are going to take me Home!"

But Trent and Paige took Sam to their home.

They showed him to their Mom and Dad,
Dad said, "He's a quarter note,
and I think he would like to sit
on the piano.....".
"That is not my home",
cried SAM ...but
they heard no sound at all.

So Sam was placed gently on the keyboard, ... and soon he went sound asleep.

The Sound of Sam

The family was all sleeping.

The Sound of Sam

SAM WOKE up.

... It was very dark in the room now, except for a moonbeam shining through the open window.

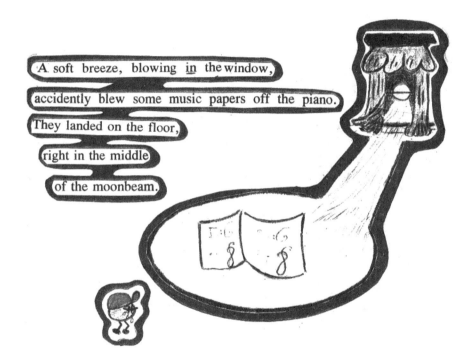

A soft breeze, blowing in the window, accidently blew some music papers off the piano. They landed on the floor, right in the middle of the moonbeam.

The Sound of Sam

SAM blinked back tears, for when he looked, he could see his whole family, some relatives, and many friends. He called out, "Here I am, it's Sam", and he jumped off the piano, onto the stool, and then to the floor.

The Sound of Sam

They all called to him to come home quickly, and take his rightful place on the paper, where he belonged.

Without his house, and doors, and extra little ledger lines, no one could hear a note.

Now he knew what he was, and why 'NO ONE' had been able to hear him.

The Sound of Sam

They explained that his sound often changed when he moved around INSIDE HIS HOUSE.

But outside his home, he was just SAM.

"That was the reason", they said,

"that your new friends,

like **Paige and Trent,** couldn't hear you.

He could sing to them now--the children, the birds, the train the owl, the breeze, (and the frog), and they could all hear him.

Sam hurried to write a letter to the children, and he pinned it to his hat.

When Paige and Trent came downstairs in the morning, SAM was gone. They looked everywhere, and finally found his hat, with a short note pinned to it.

Paige read the note to Trent. It said......

Paige and Trent:
Thank you for helping me.
I have found my family,
and they are taking me
home. When you look
at the music on your
piano, and play a song,
you will be able to hear
me.
    Goodby. Love .. SAM.

The Sound of Sam

Printed in the United States
by Baker & Taylor Publisher Services